minedition

North American edition published 2016 by mineditionUS,
an imprint of Astra Books for Young Readers, a division of Astra Publishing House

mineditionUS, 19 West 21st Street, #1201, New York, NY 10010
This book was printed in April 2022 at LEO PAPER PRODUCTS LTD.
Level 9, Telford House, 16 Wang Hoi Road, Kowloon Bay, Kowloon, Hong Kong.
Typesetting in Papyrus
Library of Congress Cataloging-in-Publication Data available upon request.

ISBN 978-988-8341-51-1
10 9 8 7 6 5 4 3

For more information please visit our website: astrapublishinghouse.com

Kate Westerlund

The Message of the Birds

with pictures by Feridun Oral

mini-minedition

The old owl began a story he had told many times over the years.

"Long ago in a simple stable, a child was born.
And as he lay, the animals of the stable tenderly watched.
And there were birds in the rafters listening to the gentle
cooing and gurgling of the baby.
But what they heard in his voice were the words of a song
that they would carry throughout the world... It was a
special song of blessing, of joy and good will."

"Why don't we sing it anymore?" asked the robin.

"People don't listen," said the partridge.

"Why not?" asked the cuckoo.

"Perhaps it is the language they no longer understand,"
said the lark.

"But if they listened with their hearts..." suggested the little
robin, "hearts understand every language, don't they?"

"Some people think the message is for others and is not meant for them," said the owl.

"I think many have had their ears closed for so long they don't remember how to listen," said the hoopoe.

"The children..." said the robin softly.

"We should sing it for the children,"
he continued. "They would listen and
they would understand the message!"

For a moment there was not a sound,
and then suddenly the branches
were alive with twittering, and chirping
and every kind of bird sound.

They all agreed.
"Tell every bird you see," the owl said.
"Tell them wherever they fly,
to whisper the message;
sing it softly to every child."

The birds flew in every direction.
Some had long journeys, but wherever they flew,
they sang and whispered to bird after bird...

...and to child after child.

Then one night it was time. A big, bright, beautiful star shone down over the earth.

A child came with a little lantern and reached out to hold the hand of another. She held the hand of her brother, and he reached for the hand of a friend.

People came with candles, lights, and torches to see
what was happening. They saw hands linked together –
white hands, brown hands, black hands.
Children everywhere were joining together.

The children
had heard the message of the birds,
and what had started as a whisper now resounded from
shining faces all over the world. For, you see, hearts do
understand every language –

"Hear us, hear the message…"

"Let there be peace.
Peace on Earth!"

taika *paco* pasch

Nyeinjanyei PACI Wolakota

Sholem **Fifa** Wetaskiwin Baris

Amani 𝔓𝔞𝔦𝔵 Sulh NANOMONSETÔTSE **béke**

ความสงบสุข سلام hòa bình *kev sib haum xeeb*

SANTIPHAP Мир **malu** FRIEDE 평화

kapayapaan *Pace* 和平 **mír** Peoning Hwa

paz sānti P E A C E *tlamatcanemiliztli* ENH TAIWAIN

Hetep Irini *fred* 平和 *Sidi* **rauha** PERDAMAIAN

Ειρήνη *vrede* Heiwa PAX Waki Qiwebis

سلام **KHANAGHUTYUN**

síocháin **Pau** שָׁלוֹם *vrede*

shAnti *Tutkium* **Rukun** Soksang *pakoj*

Spokoj *amn; salaam* **rongo** Hasiti

TSUMUKIKIATU Amaithi

uxolo *Layeni* **sërë**